CHARLIE & MOUSE & GRUMPY

By LAUREL SNYDER   Illustrated by EMILY HUGHES

chronicle books · san francisco

For Mose and Lewis, as usual.
And for Grumpy, who likes to rest his eyes —L.S.

To Aiden and Dylan —E.H.

Library of Congress Cataloging-in-Publication Data:

Names: Snyder, Laurel. | Hughes, Emily (Illustrator), illustrator.
Title: Charlie & Mouse & Grumpy / by Laurel Snyder ; illustrated by Emily Hughes.
Other titles: Charlie and Mouse and Grumpy
Description: San Francisco : Chronicle Books, [2017] |
Summary: Brothers Charlie and Mouse enjoy a special visit from Grumpy.
Identifiers: LCCN 2014026792 | ISBN 9781452137483
Subjects: LCSH: Brothers—Juvenile fiction. | Grandfathers—Juvenile fiction.
| Families—Juvenile fiction |
CYAC: Brothers—Fiction. | Grandfathers—Fiction. | Family life—Fiction.
Classification: LCC PZ7.S6851764Ci 2017 | DDC [E]—dc23
LC record available at https://lccn.loc.gov/20140267912

Manufactured in China.

Design by Kristine Brogno.
Typeset in Baskerville.
The illustrations in this book were rendered
by hand in graphite and with Photoshop.

10 9 8 7 6 5 4 3 2 1

Chronicle Books LLC
680 Second Street
San Francisco, California 94107

Chronicle Books—we see things differently.
Become part of our community at www.chroniclekids.com.

Contents

There was a knock.

At the door.

There was a knock at the door!

It was Grumpy!

"GRUMPY!"

"Charlie and Mouse!" cried Grumpy.

"You are getting so big!"

"Yes," said Charlie, "I am getting *so* big!

I can read. And swim. And eat *three* hot dogs!"

"That is a lot of hot dogs," said Grumpy.

Charlie nodded. "*With* mustard."

Mouse shook his head. "I am not getting big."

"Well," said Grumpy. "You are bigger than you

were. You are not getting small."

"No," said Mouse. "I am not getting small."

"Then what are you getting?" asked Grumpy.

Mouse thought about that.

"I am getting medium," he said.

"Aha," said Grumpy. "What is it like being

medium?"

"When you are medium," said Mouse,

"you can read *some* books. But also, people

read books to you."

"What else?" asked Grumpy.

Mouse thought again.

"When you are medium, you can swim.

But your mom sits on the steps and watches.

Just in case."

"Ahh," said Grumpy. "It sounds very nice

to be medium."

"It is," said Mouse.

"And how many hot dogs can you eat?"

 asked Grumpy. "When you are medium?"

"You can still eat three hot dogs," Mouse said.

"But *not* with mustard. Mustard is *not* medium."

"That makes sense," said Grumpy.

Grumpy carried his bag inside.

Charlie helped.

Mouse helped, too.

When they were done, Charlie said,

"Do you know what?"

"No," said Grumpy.

"No," said Mouse.

They did not know what.

"It is almost lunchtime," said Charlie.

"When it comes to hot dogs," said Grumpy,

"I am medium, too."

POUNCING

Charlie woke up.

Mouse woke up.

"Grumpy is here!" said Charlie.

"Should we pounce him?" asked Mouse.

"Of course!" said Charlie.

They snuck downstairs.

Grumpy was in the kitchen.

Grumpy was drinking coffee.

Mouse looked sad.

"Why are you sad?" Grumpy asked Mouse.

"We wanted to pounce you," said Mouse.

"So pounce me!" said Grumpy.

"We can only pounce

when you are sleeping,"

said Charlie.

"It is a rule," said Mouse.

"That makes sense," said Grumpy. "But you will

have to get up very early to catch me sleeping."

After breakfast, Charlie and Mouse

drew robots. With robot-dogs.

Grumpy sat in the armchair.

He watched Charlie and Mouse draw.

He read a book.

Then his nose began to snore.

"Grumpy?" asked Mouse.

Grumpy's nose kept snoring.

"Hey, GRUMPY!" shouted Charlie.

Grumpy sat up. "Huh? What? Wuzzat?"

Mouse laughed.

"You were taking a nap," said Charlie.

"I was *not* taking a nap," said Grumpy.

"No way."

"It *looked* like a nap," said Mouse.

"It looked a *lot* like a nap," said Charlie.

"I was just resting my eyes," said Grumpy.

"Really?" said Charlie.

"If you say so," said Mouse.

Charlie and Mouse drew robot-cats.

To go with the robot-dogs.

Grumpy's nose began to snore again.

Mouse set down his pencil.

"Charlie, do you know what I am thinking?"

said Mouse.

"Yes," said Charlie. "I do."

SONGS

Mom and Dad were missing.

Mom and Dad were on a date.

It was Grumpy night!

"GRUMPY NIGHT!"

"Who likes pizza?" asked Grumpy.

"Everyone!" said Charlie.

"With extra cheese," said Mouse.

They ate pizza.

"Who likes forts?" asked Grumpy.

"Everyone!" said Charlie.

"I'll get the flashlight," said Mouse.

They built a fort.

"Who likes movies?" asked Grumpy.

"Everyone!" said Charlie.

"But not too scary," said Mouse.

They watched a movie about

a not-too-scary dragon.

"Who likes to go to bed?" asked Grumpy.

"Now you are being silly," said Charlie.

"Nobody likes to go to bed."

"It looks like Mouse does," said Grumpy.

"That is different," said Charlie.

"He is not *in* bed."

"You are right about that," said Grumpy.

"We should take him there."

"I'll help!" said Charlie.

"Now you have to sing the good night song,"

said Charlie. "It is a rule."

"I am not a very good singer,"

said Grumpy.

"Please?" said Charlie.

"I will *try*," said Grumpy.

Grumpy sang.

23

When he was finished, Charlie said,

"You are not a very good singer, Grumpy."

"I told you so," said Grumpy.

"Also, that is not the right song," said Charlie.

"Which song is the right song?" asked Grumpy.

"Is it the one about painting ponies?"

"No, that is not the right song," said Charlie.

"Is it the one about buying a bird?" asked

Grumpy.

"No, that is not the right song," said Charlie.

"Well, is it the one about jumping in a river?"

asked Grumpy.

"No, that is not the right song either,"

said Charlie.

"I know!" said Charlie. "*I* will sing the song.

Then you will know it."

"Okay," said Grumpy.

Charlie sang.

"Can you sing it again?" asked Grumpy.

"I did not quite get it all."

Charlie sang the song again.

Most of it, anyway.

GOOD-BYE

Charlie and Mouse watched Grumpy pack.

Blanket watched, too.

They were all very quiet.

Mouse sighed. "Blanket is sad."

"Why is Blanket sad?" asked Grumpy.

"Blanket is sad because of the rain,"

said Mouse.

"Oh," said Grumpy. "I thought maybe

it was something else."

Grumpy zipped up his bag.

Mouse sighed again. "Blanket is still sad."

"Well," said Grumpy. "It is still raining."

"Yes," said Mouse. "Also, Blanket wants a cookie."

"I don't have any cookies," said Grumpy.

"I didn't think so," said Mouse.

Grumpy wheeled his suitcase away.

Charlie followed Grumpy.

Mouse followed Grumpy.

They stood at the door.

Grumpy put on his shoes.

Grumpy put on his hat.

Grumpy hugged Charlie and Mouse.

"You know," he said. "Sometimes, it has to rain. So that you can be happy when the sun comes out again. Did you ever think about that?"

Mouse thought about that.

"No," Mouse said. "Blanket would be happy if it was sunny all the time. Blanket likes the sun."

"Oh," said Grumpy. "I guess I was wrong."

Grumpy hugged Charlie and Mouse again.

Grumpy said, "Don't get too medium.

Okay, Mouse?"

Mouse nodded.

Grumpy opened the door.

Charlie said, "You know what, Grumpy?"

"What?" asked Grumpy.

"I don't think Mouse was talking about

Blanket," said Charlie. "I don't think Blanket

is the sad one."

"You don't?" said Grumpy.

"No," said Charlie. "I think he was talking

about me."

Dear Grumpy,
You forgot
your toothbrush.
XOXOXXO
Charlie + MOUSE
P.S. - come back soon